Blood Lust

L.M. Mountford

ABOUT THE AUTHOR

A self-confessed Tiger fanatic, L.M. Mountford was born and raised in England, first in the town of Bridgewater, Somerset, before later moving to the city of Gloucester where he currently resides. A fully qualified and experienced Scuba Diver, he has travelled across Europe and Africa diving wrecks and seeing the wonders of the world.

He started writing when he was 14. Under the pseudonym Dark Inferno, he has written more than thirty Fanfiction stories.

Don't Miss Out

Sign up for my newsletter and receive weekly updates on my writing progress, cover reveals, public appearances, reviews, and a FREE eBook.

That's right, a free book every week.

And, sometimes even chances to win advanced copies of my next book before anyone else. So, subscribe to my mailing list today, and keep up will all my new releases and special deals, exclusive to my inner circle.

Subscribe via my website

lmmountford.com

BloodLust

LM Mountford

Lucian

It was time.

The last light of dusk was slipping into inky black and high overhead, through the canopy of clouds and pollution, the heavens have come alive with all the magnificence of the celestial sphere. Thousands of sights no human eye could ever see.

The hour of the wolf, the time of the vampire, had come. The time to hunt, to feed...

I inhaled the backstreet in a breath and a shiver slithered down my spine at the heavy perfume of things that didn't bear contemplating. Needless to say, it was rank. Human cities often carried a certain pungency about them, so much waste and body odour, pressed together in such tight quarters, left its mark. They had gotten used to the stink and given enough time, even a vampire could adjust. But that place…

Its particular ripeness was absolutely foul.

I pressed on regardless. Lured by that single overpowering aroma that clung to this place. Beneath the stink of shit. Blood. It leads me like a carrot dangling in front of a donkey, teasing my fangs, my mouth watering.

Sooner or later, the thirst always won.

And I'd left it too long.

The way was dark but up above and all around, the city burned bright. False light. Humanity's instinctive terror of the dark and all that lurked within, cloaked by darkness, had driven them to harness the power of the sun and turn night into day. Edison's great folly. The old man had sought to create a warm light for all mankind, warmth and safety for every home. Instead, his invention had made them arrogant. Naive.

Humanity had grown careless, wrapped in their protective cocoon. So they'd forgotten the perils of the night, the hunters in the shadows and all the things that fed on them when the sun went down.

And had allowed darkness to creep back into their world.

I paused mid-stride. The trail swung off the beaten path and down the mouth of an alley a few meters ahead and I felt the instinctive thrill. I was getting close.

Men. Four of them. All in leather and denim. Huddled so close together that to any passers-by, they looked just like any other a bunch of dudes out smoking, drinking, and whiling away a night on the town. But the smell was on them. Blood and fear. It was old, maybe weeks dry, but they were rank with it. And their eyes were all fixed on the mouth of the alley, waiting.

They'd do. A small smirk tugged irresistibly at the corner of my mouth. It would be so easy.

Though they gave no outward sign of noticing me, their hearts quickened as I walked into the open, the palpitations pulsing through their clothes. Then they all turned and the biggest of the group, a brute of a man with a face like a bulldog and a spider web tattoo etched across his shaved pate, stepped forward. "Hey man!"

Spinning around, I did my best to look surprised as he pushed himself forward and walked towards me. The others fell into step, spreading to his left and right. "H-hi, can I help you?" I said, my voice shaky.

"Yeah," *Spider Web's* stride quickened, moving in for the kill. "Gotta light?" His hand was in his jean's pocket. No doubt a ploy to make me think he was reaching for his cigarettes. Idiot. He had something there. Its outline was clearly defined against the denim, but it was too long and thin to be anything like a carton of smokes. A flick knife probably. Knife crimes had been on the rise over the last couple of years. Easier to conceal than a firearm, with a considerably lower criminal sentence for carrying one if caught.

They were out of the alley and encircling me, closing in. I pivoted right then left, making a show of trying to watch them all at once, of being afraid to have my back to even one of them. "E-excuse me?"

Just a few steps closer.

"Hey, he asked you a question," the one to my right asked, a lanky black, all smiles and teeth and-

My eyes narrowed on him. Something was wrong. He smelled wrong, like meat just starting to rot. Corruption. Disease.

I shifted my focus back to Spider Web. Dogs followed the alpha, the biggest and strongest of their pack. Bullies and cowards followed the same logic. He would give them orders. And the corruption was heaviest in him. And that could only mean one thing.

My hunger promptly dried up. I'm not the fussiest vampire, but I do have some standards. Feeding off of scum was all well and good, however, killers and rapists riddled with venereal diseases were about as appetising as mouldy bread.

Promptly dropping the farce, I turned on my heel and moved on.

"Hey! I asked if you 'ave a light!" Spider Web shouted, and I half expected him to come after me. "Fucker, I'm talking to you!"

The pair on my left barred my way. One dark, short, and squat with arms corded in muscle. The other tall and doughy with lank blonde hair. They looked a right comical sight with their arms crossed, standing the sort of straight-backed posture a bouncer might adopt to look tough barring a club door. They were more Del and Rodney Trotter than Ronnie and Reggie Kray and as I closed the distance, Del Boy made to grab my arm.

"Touch me, and I'll take your arm and beat you to death with it," I promised, my voice low and deadly serious, but loud enough for all the group to catch every word.

The Trotter brothers promptly stepped back.

"What are you doin', no- stop, fucker, come back here…" Impotent, Spider Web could do little more than hurl obscenities

at my back, like a child whose mother had just taken his favourite toy away. Eventually, they're swallowed by the night and I went on, all the more famished but with nothing to show for the experience.

Then I heard it. Low and far away, but unmistakable.

Unsure of what else I might find lurking amidst warren of 'abandoned' warehouses, I followed it cautiously. At first, it was little more than a thrumming beat in the air, but it grew with every step, leading me down to an old, dilapidated structure sitting just on the river. With its windows bricked over, parts of the roof missing or stolen, and red brick walls well decorated with layers of graffiti, it would have almost certainly been condemned long ago. No doubt, whatever developer had secured the plot would be chomping at the bit to tear it down and turn it into an extension of the outlet megastore across the water. Demolition notices already adorned most of the surrounding buildings.

The booming music emanating from within indicated that it was not entirely deserted. Walking around the parameter, I found the entrance to an old subterranean coal bunker near the edge of the water. A padlock dangled off one rusted handle, unlocked and undoubtedly the entrance to whatever party raged inside.

The door opened smoothly, despite the rust, onto a gentle slope of the bunker's coal chute. Thick layers of black coal dust lined the walls so I'm careful not to touch anything as I edged down the slope. It's a tight fit, just barely wide enough for me to shuffle through. In its day, this would have been filled by river steamers or bargeman selling and shipping coal up and down the water to power the warehouse's great machines. With the passing of the fossil fuels however, it had obviously been converted into a dumping ground and squatter site.

Rubbish bags. Shopping trolleys. Drugs and other such paraphernalia. You name it, it had it.

The only door leading to and from the bunker was all the easier to see by the slivers of light between it and the frame.

I knocked, and a doorman answered, slowly pulling it open but barring my entry with his impressive bulk. More than six feet of muscle, he had to outweigh me by more than five stone, a mass that his black and white striped top struggled to contain.

He sneered down at me. "Members only."

"So I see." I glanced at the nearest pile of rubbish bags. "Discerning clientele?"

His sneer twisted. "Very."

"And if I want to become a member?"

"Not accepting new members." He seemed to be having difficulty keeping the smugness from his voice. "But if you give me thirty quid, I'll let you in with a guest pass."

"Ah, and if I happen to of left my wallet at home?"

"Then I'm afraid I'm going to have to ask you to leave, sir. Where would you like to land."

"Oh, I don't think that will be necessary." It certainly would have been fun watching this brute try to strong-arm me out, but time was of the essence and that sort of struggle would have drawn too much attention from the denizens within. Instead, I simply looked him in the eye.

It took all of seconds. All brawn and no brains, the doorman refused to look away, yet was no match in a battle of wills and visibly quelled, until all defiance had fled him. "Of course, sir." He conceded, shuffling back like a whipped dog with his tail between his legs "Welcome."

I walked past without sparing the weak-minded fool a second glance, into the warehouse's interior. It was massive, three stories tall with catwalks running along the second and third that had been converted into frames for the speakers and lighting. Amidst the gaggle of perilously thin bodies dancing around a performing DJ, a mass of dusty old crates and plywood lengths had been fitted together to serve as a makeshift bar. Old and well-used tables and chairs were haphazardly scattered around, the sort you might find at a cheap DIY store sale and were likely to collapse the moment you started to get comfortable.

The atmosphere practically buzzed with energy and sexual tension.

I circled the floor twice, weaving in and out amongst the bodies, taking the time to admire some of the choicer morsels as I went, their tight young bodies writhing to whatever beat pulsed through the sound system, adorned in as few garments as possible, hearts racing, blood pulsing. It had me practically salivating at the thought of plunging my fangs into their milky-

Then I forget all the rest, my eyes locked on a stark and desolate beauty, seated on the edge of the crowd. Detached and alone in a sea of life.

The first glimpse of her had me at first doubting my own eyes. She certainly didn't have the look of someone you'd usually find frequenting a shithole like this.

Dressed in jeans and a red long-sleeved turtleneck, there was nothing showy or made up about her. The beauty was all her own. And she was beautiful, with soft, delicate features and diamond blue eyes framed by long flowing curls, dark and lustrous as ravens' wings. But there was more. Behind that girl next door exterior. An edge. A stiffness. A haunted tension that never should belong in one so young.

Hmm… interesting. Resisting the impulse to walk straight over to her, I detoured over to the bar and ordered a drink. All the while keeping one eye fixed on the girl at the table.

At its heart, the hunt was nothing more than a game. It could be played with subtlety or like a bull in a china shop. The latter was easier, but far less satisfying, or fun. And where would we be without a little fun now and then?

"That'll be a tenner, mate."

I glanced back. The bartender, a greasy guy with enough oil in his hair for it to shimmer and dance with colour beneath the laser lights, stood over me, an impatient look on his face and a clear drink in a dirty plastic glass waited on the bar.

I looked from him to the drink, then back to him. "You've got to be kidding me, it's not even half full."

"Too bad, that's all we have." He makes no effort to hide the kegs and bottles stacked behind the bar. "Don't like it fine, piss off. But you gotta pay."

"Really?"

"Yea, really-" I looked him in the eye and the words die in his throat. "Well, um… of course, I can set up a slate for you. Yes, I'll get a slate put in your name, Mr… oh it doesn't matter, I'll just put down my name, no problem…". He turned and scurried off out of my sight.

"Pathetic."

Not bothering to watch his retreat, I reached into my jacket and took the hip flask I kept on hand out of the breast pocket. Careful to ensure no one was watching, I unscrewed the lid and poured the contents into the drink, so it turned a deep shade of rose, before returning the flask to its hideaway.

Turning back to watch the girl, I couldn't resist the smile that tugged at my mouth, revealing the hint of a fang. She was very, very lovely…

"Is this seat taken?"

She whirled around, eyes widening at the sight of me looming over her. I had to force back my toothy grin. She looked like a scared little rabbit. A rabbit with the most beautiful eyes I'd ever seen.

"Um, I suppose so." Her voice trembled but I'd already pulled the seat back and had made myself comfortable. She looked away quickly, her heart already racing, those big blue eyes flitting back and forth, desperate for something, anything to look at other than me. *Good, I'm already affecting her. This may just be easier than I thought. A few more little pushes and this delicate little rabbit will be all mine.*

And she would be mine.

"I'm Lucian," I said, taking a sip of my drink, just slow enough for her eyes to focus on my mouth.

I could practically feel her heart fluttering as her eyes lingered just that moment too long. Then she pulled herself together and hurriedly looked away. "Kate."

"Beautiful." I smiled. "Such a beautiful name for such a beautiful girl. But a beauty by any other name would be no less exquisite." I extended my hand.

Uncertain, her eyes moved from my hand, to my face, back down to my hand, then back to the sea of bodies rippling around us.

"Would you prefer *come here often?*" I dropped my hand. "How about what's a nice girl like you doing in a dive like this?"

"Is that the best you've got?" She said it without looking, but the tension in her voice betrayed her. She was interested, and she was overcompensating to try and resist my *charms*.

"Oh, my dear girl, you have no idea." This was going to be easier than I thought. "You're not waiting for anyone, by any chance, are you? I'd hate to interrupt."

Her head whipped around, eyes suddenly bright. "What makes you think I'm-"

"Such beauty should never be unaccompanied," I smirked across my drink at her before making a show of looking past her. "And by the way you keep watching all these people, I'd say you're looking for someone."

Kate visibly relaxed. "What sharp little eyes you've got."

"I have my *talents*, just wait till you get to my teeth." She blushed and dropped her eyes to the table. "So," I pressed, "who's the lucky fellow?"

"It's just a friend."

"A friend?"

"Yes," She sipped her otherwise untouched drink. A Henry, judging by the strong smell of citrus. "She's been badgering me all week to come to this party and barely ten minutes after we get through the door, she disappears."

She was lying.

She had a talent for deception for sure. Her story was simple and plausible, her delivery perfect. If I had been anyone else, she might very well of pulled the wool over my eyes. But she could not lie to me. I could tell, I could always tell.

Nevertheless, I played along. "Good friends are hard to come by. Would you care for some company till she gets back?"

"N-no, it's fine." She drained her drink. "I saw her going off with some guy a little while ago. No doubt she'll have him balls deep by now and will have completely forgotten about me. So, I'll be leaving soon."

"For home?"

"Yes."

"Is it far?"

"Far Enough."

"Do you drive?"

She scowled. "I don't think that's any of your business."

Her anger only inflamed my amusement and desire. There was some fire in my little rabbit after all. "The city's no safe place for a girl all alone. If you're not driving, I wouldn't dream of letting you walk home all alone. Anything could happen."

At my words, Kate sucked in a breath. Suddenly she was as white as a sheet.

"No, thank you. I'll be fine." She pushed back from the table, grabbing her clutch as she got to her feet. "Nice to meet you, Mr Lucian." Then she was gone into the crowd.

I watched her go, unable to resist admiring the way her jeans hugged the curves of her buttocks as she sashayed through the bodies. I couldn't wait to sink my fangs into that luscious derrière. "The pleasure, I'm sure, will be all mine."

Kate

The body lay on the cold steel table for me to identify. A white sheet covered him, but it had been pulled back to below his chin, but just above the red smile cut from ear to ear.

The face was a ruin. Once so lean and handsome, the thing before me is black and blue and swollen with cuts and bruises. More a haunch of rotten and beaten meat than a man. And the blood, so much blood.

I couldn't bear to look. He was unrecognisable, yet I knew. I knew this was him. I knew this was David.

I knew this was my brother.

I forced myself not to run as unshed tears burned the corners of my eyes.

Anything can happen. Yea I suppose he was right about that. There were monsters out there, monsters who'd stolen the only person I had left.

I walked without thinking, letting my feet lead me wherever. Anywhere. I didn't care, I just needed to keep walking. Until…

Until what? They found me? I thought they'd find me in that shithole. They'd found David there, or at least that's what the police thought. Evidence had been lacking. Witnesses unwilling to come forward.

They didn't care. No one cared about one dead boy raped and butchered in a gutter.

But I cared.

He was my brother, and I wanted the bastards who did that to him.

But instead, I'd found him. Or rather he'd found me. Lucian.

Just the memory of him made my belly flutter.

There was something off about him, I just couldn't put my finger on it. He was just too swarve, in that old fashioned, debonair, Jane Austen and Mr Darcy sort of way. From the moment he opened his mouth, he had just exuded charm. And that face, all sharp lines and smooth planes, he was a work of art carved from pristine white marble with black pearl eyes glinting out from beneath tumbles of thick jet-black hair just that bit too long it begged for a hand to run through it. He was the very embodiment of dark and dangero-

I froze, a cold cascade sloshing down my spine. What was that?

"Hey babe, you lost?" A man's voice, deep and guttural called from behind me, close. Very close.

Swallowing, I turned and found myself surrounded.

"A hot little dish like you must be pretty stupid to be walking around this neighbourhood all alone," the body that came with the voice was immense, a big thuggish brute with a spider's web tattooed on his bald head. "You a ho looking for work?" The others all gave him space as he stepped forward, like mangy dogs backing from the alpha. "Well we don't pay for cunt, ho, ya hear me, we fuck it. Ya hear that boys, we fuck it till it's broke!"

They all began to snigger and lick their lips at that, and my hand dropped down to my clutch, its familiar weight giving me strength.

The black guy on my left stepped forward, grinning with a set of large pure white teeth. "Where's your pimp ho? Little bitches shouldn't wander the streets all alone. Anything could of happened..." He stepped in close, one hand brushing over my shoulders to scoop up my hair. He brought it up to his nose and sniffed, making me shiver with revulsion. "Good thing we found you."

"Yeah, anything coulda' happened." The giant grinned as the two to my right closed the gap. "Don't worry, you're safe now. This is our neighbourhood." I'd been snared like a mouse in a trap.

It was them. I knew it. I couldn't explain how, but I just knew.

"And nothing happens on your streets without your say so." My voice came out as cool as ice and I had to keep my fist clenched around my clutch to keep from shaking.

"Ya could say that, yea."

"Did you do it?" I knew this beast killed David, but I needed to hear it. Hear him say it, confess.

"Do wha?"

I saw red. How could he not know? The black guy was tall. Much taller than me. And the way he was trying to cover my back to keep me from running away left him completely open so that when I jammed my elbow back, it hit the one place it would do the most damage.

His grunt caught them all off guard. They'd expected me to run, to plead and beg. Never to attack. So they were too late to stop my hand as it slipped into my clutch.

They all stepped back when I pulled out the Browning Hi-Power Mark I.

It had been my father's old service pistol, he'd carried it through his national service. I'd found it buried amongst his things whilst I was clearing out their house after their funeral. I'd kept it along with a few other mementoes and forgotten all about it until tonight.

"Two months ago!" I snapped, raising the pistol so the business end pointed straight for the giant's torso. "A boy was murdered here! Did you do it?"

"You talking crazy girl!" one of the men shouted, but I didn't look at him. My eyes were set on the giant. He looked too calm, like he didn't care, but his eyes. They burned with fury. I had drawn a gun on him and that enraged him. How dare I; this was his neighbourhood, his street, and I had the nerve to pull a piece. Good, let the bastard squirm, he should know what it felt like. He'd made David suffer in the worst possible ways. Well, I would make him pay. For my brother.

"What makes you think we had anything to do with it?" Another voice shouted. The black guy, I guessed. Good, none of his friends were coming to help him, he was alone, and he didn't like it.

"It happened here in your neighbourhood."

"Bitch, please! That was talk. Just talk. We had nothing to do with it."

"Yea, po-po would have been all over us."

"Bullshit!" I spat it out, all ice and fire. They did it. I knew they did. They murdered my brother!

"Yea, it's bullshit, sweetheart" the giant growled.

"You killed him?"

"Yea. Little cunt wouldn't shut his fucking mouth, so I opened his throat. Whatcha gonna do about it? Shoot me?"

"Yeah."

"Bitch, you ain't got the minerals." He laughed, a deep grizzled laugh that sent ice straight through my belly. "Go on then, blow me away in cold blood. They'll stick a mad ho like you in some dyke slam to eat fanny for twenty years. Bet you'd like that, wouldn't you, all the pussy you can eat. They'll be lining up to get a piece of you. So, go ahead if you're serious, shoot me, shoot me, shoot-"

I pulled the trigger.

I had expected a bang, for the Browning to kick back as they did in the movies. But all that came out was a click. A dull metallic click no louder than a whisper, but at that moment it bellowed like a clap of thunder.

Ice rushed through my veins. My eyes dropped to the pistol, then back up to the giant and I tried again. And again.

Nothing.

He smiled, a cruel twisted thing, like barbed wire wound into knots across his face. "Works better with the safety off."

He grabbed the Browning, his immense paw encompassing the barrel, and wrenched it out of my hand.

I didn't have time to scream. One moment I'd been standing there, the next I'd been pressed up against a wall, hard enough to drive the breath from my lungs, with one of them driving his arms against my neck while the others pawed at my clothes.

Panic and bile leapt into my throat. Gasping, fighting for breath, I tried to push the arm away, but the giant thwarted my efforts and pinned my arms above my head. He applied just enough pressure for my joints to scream in protest, and for a single heart-stopping moment, I thought he might break both my arms.

No, this can't be happening. Hot angry tears burned my eyes, yet I fought the pain that seared up my arms and lashed out. My knee hit something soft, and one of them grunted and cursed for his balls. I would have laughed, but I was too swamped with the instinctive need to flee, to escape, to make that desperate break for it.

The fight left me however when a titanic force slammed into my stomach. I went limp, the pain enough that I would have doubled over, but the restraining arm held me where I was.

"Hold still you little bitch." A voice hissed. "The more you resist, the worse this gets for you."

A roll of duct tape appeared, and a hand wound the binding round and round my wrists, to the point all circulation was cut off and my fingers began to tingle.

The giant stepped in to dominate my view, my father's Browning raised and pointed at my face. "Go on, look. Look down the barrel, you see the bullet?"

I could. The muzzle was black, much too dark to see down. But I could see the bullet well enough all the same.

"Answer me, can you see it?"

"Yes." And so much more.

I could smell the gun pounder, filling my nostrils in thick grey clouds, acrid and pungent against the night air. I heard the bang of the shot, saw my head snap back, my face a ruin. And red, so much red. Red smoke, red pulp and bone, a red cloud, and red blood everywhere.

"Good now open wide. I want you to suck it. Come on, suck it."

A part of me tried to be brave, screamed for me to tell them to go to hell and then shut my mouth tight. But the fear pulsed through me, making me shake, and hot tears rolled down my cheeks as, bit by bit, my mouth opened.

"Yeah, good girl. Your brother was an obedient bitch too. I fucked him bloody then handed him round to the rest of the boys, and when they were done, I cut his throat. If he hadn't been such a good little whore, I'd have cut his dick off and fed it to him. And if you try to run, I'll cut your tits off and-"

A deep growl rumbled through the night.

"What the fuck?" The giant lurched back and through the tears, I saw a dog padding towards us. A very big dog. All black and shaggy, like a Game of Thrones Direwolf, only not quite so cute and cuddly.

And I was almost positive it was looking at me. Then, it dipped its head, ears pricked, and fur raised, and growled another warning. It reverberated off the brick walls and shivered through flesh and bone.

"What's that?" one man asked, fear evident in his voice as he sized up the canine.

"Just a mutt," the giant shrugged, surveying the dog warily before turning his icy glare back to me. I shrunk under his gaze. "What, you'd pass up this fine piece of ass just because a mangy stray barks at ya a little."

"Well, that's a pretty big fucking stray, mate. Jesus, look at those teeth…"

The dog snapped a warning and the black guy turned and ran, tripping and stumbling over his own feet as he went.

"All right, that thing is starting to piss me off," Web turned to the two remaining men. "Del! Jake! Skin the fucker."

They both looked at each other, sharing a look like they were about to piss themselves there and then. Then they nodded, and turned to the dog. I saw a flash of silver as they pulled flick knives from the depths of their coats.

I couldn't look, couldn't watch them butcher the poor creature. I could hear the dog growling and the men's footsteps echoing, then silence. No howls or moans of agony from the dog as it was murdered. No grunts and growls from the men as they got off on killing my canine defender. Just an eerie quiet.

The silence cut deeper than their knives ever could. And it was almost a relief when the two thuds, the unmistakable sound of bodies hitting the ground-

Wait, two thuds?

I opened my eyes and could only stare at Del and Jake's dismembered bodies lying on the ground, pools of blood spreading out around them. But there was no dog.

Lucian stood over them, his pitiless eyes fixed on the giant.

And I don't know if I should laugh or scream.

"What the fuck?" The big man stuttered, his voice warbling in terror as he moved away from me, releasing his grip on my wrists. Visibly shaking, he turned my father's Browning on Lucian. "Bastard!"

My screams mingled with the crack of the shots as bloody mists burst from Lucian's back. The first should have killed him. It went clean through his heart. The second and third took him in the gut. Yet Lucian remained standing, taking each hit without so much as a grunt. Shot after shot, bullet by bullet.

"Jesus Christ, what the hell are you?" Eyes bright with panic, the giant stepped forward and cupped the pistol in both hands, raising it up for a finishing shot like they did in the movies.

It happened almost too quickly for the eye to see. One moment Lucian had been standing there, dark and pale and devastatingly intense and handsome. Out of reach and without a hope of dodging the shot. Then the Browning was arcing through the air, along with one of the hands that grasped it.

And Lucian stood over the giant.

Lucian

Say what you like about undead fiends, no one can accuse me of not being a vampire of my word.

I didn't bother to pretend I was not enjoying myself. There was something so very satisfying in being the servant of justice.

Seizing the paretic piece of filth by the scruff of the neck, I heaved him up one handed. Big and brawny, he must have weighed more than 18 stone of pure muscle, but in my grasp, he was little more than a child. His remaining hand fumbled for his knife, but it was of little consequence. That butter knife would have served him no better than it had his dead friends.

"W-w-what are you?" he choked out the words.

The stain of blood was thick in the air and I knew I should feed while there was still some life in his veins, but the thought of feeding on *that*. It was enough to turn the stomach.

"I'm hungry."

His eyes widening, Web screamed and the metallic scent teasing my fangs was suddenly cut by acid. He'd pissed himself.

One swipe was all it took. The screams died in a gurgle as I tore out his throat and dumped his carcass to the ground, to rot with the rest of the filth.

When the last of his life's blood had bled away, I turned to Kate, but she had slumped to the ground. Head back. Eyes glazed.

I felt a momentary spark of concern, however a quick check revealed that she had only fainted. Hardly surprising really, given what she had just witnessed. Shredding her bonds, I traced my thumb down her jawline and to her neck, fingering the pulse of her veins pumping hot blood just beneath the surface of her skin.

I mustn't leave her here. If the law found her there, they would likely try to pin all the deaths on her. *Girl slays three, possible self-defence*, made a much better story in the papers than *murdering vigilante on the loose, police baffled*. If she tried to tell them what she saw, they'd just stick her in a madhouse. And if she didn't, if by some miracle she got away, she'd probably end up there anyway.

She'd seen what lurked in the shadows, up close and in vivid gory detail. She might never get another night's sleep again.

Or she might not live to see the dawn.

"Ahhh little rabbit, you're proving to be a lot more trouble than I bargained for." Rising to my feet, I scooped Kate into my arms and think of home. "Typical woman."

Together our bodies slipped into mist.

Kate

It was as if I was awakening from a dream.

Blinking through the blurriness, I found myself lying on an antique sofa in a large open room that was all leather, stone, and timber. High ceilings. Oil paintings and ancient tapestries upon the walls. Timber furnishings. It was as if someone had built a medieval fortress straight from the pages of history, and it all culminated in the lord's chair in the centre of the room. A high wingback. A leather cushioned throne.

Lucian sat in it like he was born to that chair, eased back with one leg crossed, drinking a tumbler of ruby red, a man completely at ease and in control of his surroundings. The master of all he surveyed.

Except he was no man.

He was watching me. He didn't show it, but I could feel his eyes on me, observing my every move the way a wolf eyed a deer.

Panic's cold fingers encircled my heart. *Oh God. Where am I?*

There were three doors in sight, but all were too far away. I'd never make it to one before he'd be upon me, and even if I could, I had no way of knowing which led out of this place. The only window was closed and opened out into blackness. *How*

*high could we be? Almost certainly too high for me to survive
the fall but would that matter if-*

"Ah!" I screamed and almost fell over the back of the sofa in
fright as Lucian seemed to just materialise before my eyes, so
close we were almost nose to nose. I'd never seen anyone move
so fast. Hell, I hadn't even seen him moving so fast. It was as if
he'd moved faster than light. But that was impossible, wasn't it?

He put a calming hand on my shoulder. His expression was
impassive, but there was warmth in his eyes. It soothed my
panic. "Shhh…You're safe. You fainted, I brought you here to
rest until you recovered."

I had to fight to keep my fear from my voice. "And you
couldn't take me to a hospital because-"

"They ask too many questions."

I swallowed. "What are you?" Each word was like a stone in
my throat as my belly twisted in dread of the answer.

"I think you know."

"Say it," I pressed him. "Tell me!"

"A vampire."

And there it was. The answer I had been expecting, dreading,
and craving.

It was ridiculous of course, and if I hadn't *seen* him, I'd have
thought he was off his meds. But I had seen him, and I believed
it. I believed him. I believed my eyes and what I'd seen.

"And you killed those men."

"Three of them, yes. The fourth ran, but he won't get far." He
said it like it was something as every day as remarking on the
weather.

"Good." I made no effort to keep the satisfaction from my
voice.

He arched a brow. He might have taught the move to Roger
Moore himself, it was as natural to him as a bird taking to the
air. "Good?"

"They murdered my brother."

His lips pressed together and curled in one corner. "Your
welcome."

"So, what now? Are you going to…" I trailed off, unsure of
how to put the question into words.

"Feed on you?" He asked. "Yes."

I swallowed, my mouth suddenly dry. "You're going to kill
me?"

He laughed at that. He threw his head back and laughed. It should have pissed me off, but despite myself, I was immediately enthralled to the sound. He laughed like my one question was the funniest thing he'd ever heard, and it was as far from the cackling horror movie stereotype as it was possible to be. It was full and deep and rolled over me like a warm hand brushing down my back, the fingers playing my spine.

I could have listened to that sound for the rest of my days, but his humour dried up as suddenly as it had come. "Why would I kill you?"

"But you said-"

"I'd feed on you, yes."

"That makes no sense," I said, and I felt my face screw up in confusion, my cheeks growing hot with embarrassment. I felt like a child in a difficult class, with a teacher who only spoke in riddles. "How can you feed on me and not kill me?"

"At any time, there is enough blood in a human body to quench my thirst more than five times over. I don't need to take your life to survive, just some of your blood."

"So, you've never..."

"Killed to feed?" Lucian said before slowly getting up from his chair and walking over to a stone mini bar. "On occasion. But they deserved their fate, like our mutual friends tonight." From a selection of crystals, he picked the brandy decanter and refilled his tumbler with a deep ruby red. "Of course, there are some that make a habit of it, but that runs its own risks. The Vampire Council takes a dim view of drawing necessary attention to our kind."

"A vampire council? There's a council made up of vampires out there?"

"Yes, the elders. The oldest and strongest of us. They rule the vampire nation from its seat of power in London."

"Vampire Nation! How many of you are there?"

"Thousands."

"Thousands." I parroted, not quite sure I had heard him right.

"Yes, thousands." I could feel myself getting warm from the amusement in his tone, like he was humouring an inquisitive child, full of endless questions. "I dare say you've seen some, maybe even spoken to a few of my kind before. Once vampires had to be cunning to survive, but it is so easy to blend in now. We need only a set of fangs. And a little charm."

"But, what about sunlight? You'll die if you go out in broad daylight!"

"Just a myth." He sat down beside me on the sofa, and I didn't recoil. I don't know what it was about him, but he seemed to exert a pull that made me want to be closer to him the longer I spent in his company. It was strange, but also kind of nice. "Vampires are extremely sensitive to ultraviolet light. It will weaken us, even burn if one doesn't feed regularly. But fatal, no." He grimaced as he took his first drink from the glass. "Err, cloned blood has its uses, but it tastes like shit."

It was meant as a joke, I knew, a poor attempt at humour to ease the tension that had amassed between us, but I was beyond such things now.

"Can I see them- y-your fangs I mean, can I see them, please?" My voice faltered but I stayed firm, desperate for something, anything to focus my attention on.

If my request surprised him, Lucian gave no sign. He watched me over his tumbler for a moment, and I knew he was thinking the proposition over. That pissed me off. What, did he think I was a silly little girl who couldn't take it? If I could stand the thought of him drinking my blood, I could take this.

He must have come to the same conclusion because he eventually put the tumbler down on the coffee table, looked at me, grinned a wide grin, and – there they were.

They came down slowly, his canines lengthening, sharpening. I watched, entranced, my heart quickening until they were fully unsheathed, deadly sharp and pearly white. And I couldn't resist. Before he could draw them back, I reached out and brushed my thumb over the white. It was sharper than it looked, like running my finger down a steak knife, and I didn't even notice I'd been cut till I saw the blood.

It rolled down my finger in fat beads and left a thick red smear. The sight had my mouth running dry, but before I could pull my arm back, Lucian had seized my wrist. His grip was firm, his fingers like iron tentacles as they wrapped around me, holding me where I was as he kissed my cut. I shuddered in pleasure, his decadent mouth working its magic, stirring me to into a fervour as he sucked my thumb, his eyes burning into mine.

Panting, my voice trembling and heart pounding, I asked "H-how will you do it?"

"However you desire." He purred and released my finger. The cut had healed. "I'll bite you of course, but the rest is up to you." Slowly, delicately, he touched his thumb to my neck and stroked back and forth, his touch cool but stirring. "The carotid artery works well but any of the major blood vessels will suffice." He stroked that single digit down my arm, the pad of his thumb raising goosebumps wherever it touched. Then taking my wrist in hand, he brought it up to his lips. He kissed the skin and I bit back a gasp of pain at the sudden sting as a fang punctured deep and ruby blood welled around his lips.

This time I could actually feel him drinking me in, tasting every bit of me, but then something soft and silky brushed over the wound and sent a rush of tingles through my nerves straight down to the pit of my tummy. It made me hot, hot enough to push my thighs together, desperate to quench the needy ache massing there.

When he lifted his head, my skin was unblemished. "The ulnar artery is best for a quick snake, but I prefer the femoral artery. The food there is so much sweeter, and just the act of feeding there can give the strongest orgasms…"

Suddenly I was in his lap. I should have been outraged but I could only moan in sweet ecstasy as his mouth dropped down to my neck, kissing, licking, ravishing me with his vampiric hunger.

He was done talking, he had tasted my blood and now he wanted more. But I needed to ask him one last thing, so I forced the words out. "Mmm… will I – oh God- will I, will I turn?"

He didn't even bother to raise his mouth from me. "Only if you want to."

And then we were done talking. His mouth took mine with a hunger, stealing all logic and reason from my mind. His kiss was rougher than what I had expected, but when he tugged at my bottom lip with his teeth, I knew I would learn to like it. I felt hot and needy, and I yielded to him as he pulled me to him, his tongue coaxing my mouth open with lush creases across my bottom lip that had the embers of my desire blazing into a wildfire.

My tummy flipped excitedly as he stood up, his fingers biting deliciously into my rump as he supported my weight, crushing me to him. My hands lost themselves in his hair as his tongue ravished my mouth, swirling round and round my own in a dance that had my toes curling. Then we were moving…

No, not moving. Floating!

The feeling lasted for a moment. I caught only a glimpse of our surroundings, swirling by, pale and ethereal, as if we were enveloped in a cloud, passing through walls and rooms alike. Then I was on my back, on the largest bed I've ever seen, with Lucian poised above me. He looked so smug; like he had me just where he wanted.

I switched our positions with a hard shove. He didn't resist and as I pushed him over, I rolled with him, swinging a leg across his hips to straddle him.

"Now then, Mr Lucian. Just lie back. This won't hurt a bit."

He watched my movements and his smile turned positively amused. "Mmm… a little bit of pain isn't necessarily a bad thing…"

A shiver ran down my spine as I noted how his eyes glittered in the low light, their onyx depths a rich ruby black. Leaning down, I lightly kissed each of his eyelids in turn. "You have beautiful eyes." I sighed, grinning as I felt the way he shivered as my breath licked across his cool skin.

I kissed his nose, then his cheeks, then his chin, maintaining as much contact as possible. My hair brushed his bare neck and he groaned softly as it tickled him. I sighed again, hardly daring to believe that it was all real, that it was happening. It was all so sudden yet felt so right. He was a vampire, but he'd saved my life. He'd murdered to protect me. Our chemistry was undeniable, and I couldn't help that feeling, the feeling of being drawn to another person. Irresistibly, overwhelmingly, beguilingly, and seductively drawn, like a helpless moth to a sexy vampiric flame.

I dropped a kiss on his jaw before sweeping my tongue up the curve of it, lightly teasing the spot beneath his ear. Slightly salty and sweet, the taste of him spread across my tongue and I shuddered. I needed more, so I began to kiss and nibble his neck. I barely noticed as his hands reached up and buried themselves in my hair.

With a fiery passion, I explored Lucian with my mouth. My tongue mapped the curve of his collarbone as my fingers urgently worked to divest him of his shirt. My lips trailed the slope of his shoulder and the hard contours of his chest. His wounds were gone, the gunshots he'd received healed and vanished. There were no scars, no blemishes. He was perfect, a block of ice, chiselled and sculpted and wrapped in skin. I licked along each ridge, using my teeth to tug gently at his flat nipples as I travelled his body.

I was lost in the taste and feel of him, in the sounds of his soft panting breaths and groans.

A gentle tug of my hair suddenly brought me back to reality and I lifted my head obediently to meet Lucian's glazed eyes.

"I watched Troy burn, heard Pompei's screams swallowed up, walked the plagued streets of London and battled werewolves and fairies and elves alike, but keep doing that, and that wicked little mouth of yours might just be what finishes me off for good." The vampire's voice was low and strained, and I couldn't help a smile of satisfaction as a feeling of immense pride filled me at the knowledge that I could elicit such a reaction.

"I won't let it kill you." My smile grew as I dragged my hands down his chest, letting my nails scrape over his delicious pale skin. He hissed a long, sharp sound that made a shiver run down my spine as my nail drew over his nipple.

Taken by an idea, I bent down and blew against the scratched area. The sound deepened and turned into a low groan. I continued to blow against his nipple until his eyes fluttered shut, then I dropped my mouth down and slid my tongue over his flesh. His eyes flew open and he bucked up against me. Keeping our eyes locked together, I bit down and then pulled back to blow, making Lucian growl as he bucked his hips up against mine again. We both moaned as our bodies ground together.

Pulling back from his chest, I worked my way down the quivering flesh of his stomach to his abdomen, stopping only to gently kiss his navel before I dipped my tongue into his belly button. I felt brazen. His hips jerked at the contact and his erection brushed the full swell of my breasts as he dropped his head back against the pillow. Curious, I looked down and contemplated the very impressive bulge in his jeans for a moment. Admiring its already remarkable girth, I took a deep breath as I slid further down his legs.

"May I?" I asked in a teasingly girlish voice, fingering small patterns over his jeans, tracing his outline.

Beyond words, Lucian could only nod, so I sat between his legs. My fingers shook as I undid the button of his jeans, but I pushed on and tugged them down his muscular legs. He raised his hips to help me get them all the way off but couldn't help moaning in relief as his desire sprang free.

My eyes fixed on his arousal and my belly fluttered with nervous excitement while heat seared my veins. I couldn't resist licking my lips like the cat who'd found the canary. Though I had little in the way of prior experience to compare him to, I knew immediately that no normal would match the example standing rampant before my eyes. He was a very big boy.

Tilting my head to the side, I reached out and ran my fingers up his cock from its base, buried in a light nest of dark hair, to the mushroom-shaped tip.

Lucian

Trying to relax, I closed my eyes against the vision of Kate between my legs as her fingers wrapped around the length of my cock. I groaned as my shaft pulsed in her grasp. Her thumb pressed on my sensitive tip and she started to stroke, her palm gliding from base to head. I barely held onto coherent thought as she began to pick up the pace, my hips rolling to meet her hand-

My eyes shot open as I felt something warm and wet wrap around the head of my cock and I could only watch as Kate sucked me, her eyes big and cheeks hollowing. I had to fight against the almost overwhelming urge to buck up into her mouth, so I seized fistfuls of the bedsheets to stop my hands from fisting her mass of curls.

"Oh shit, mmm…Kate!" I moaned, and she gave me what I wanted, taking all of me into her sinful mouth. I was so hard at that moment, so aroused that just the feeling of her breath wafting over my cock was enough to push me to the edge as she drew back.

She took her time. It was obvious that this was all new to her, but she had the general idea and wasn't afraid to try new things. I could feel her teeth pressing in and drawing back, her tongue fluttering, stroking the underside. She altered speed, angle, depth, testing, trying to find the things that brought me closer to the brink. One of Kate's hands encircled the base, massaging the exposed skin of my shaft with her forefinger and her thumb as she continued bobbing her head. It became all too much. God, no woman had ever been able to drive me this mad.

Kate must have felt my release coming on. As much as I tried to suppress it, my body was shaking, and my cock was twitching. Wrapping her lips around my head, she sucked hard while jerking me vigorously.

"Oh God, Kate!" Her name left my lips in a gasp as I went over the edge, and I could feel my release exploding into her mouth in thick jets. She swallowed it greedily, sucking me dry and not missing a drop. I came harder than I could ever remember, and the force of it left black spots dancing before my eyes. And it left me thirsty, very thirsty.

That drink at the bar had taken the edge off, but the taste of her blood had almost undone me. Now, I needed to taste her again.

By the time the spots had passed, my little rabbit was perched above me. Her lips were pursed, her eyes hooded. She looked so very pleased with herself. She was also still fully dressed, while I had allowed her to divest me of all garments.

It was time to correct that.

"That was… well… most delightful." Before Kate could react, I had her on her back. She bounced when she landed on the bed and I pushed her further into the mattress and her head sank into the pillows. Yes, this was where she belonged. Under me, in my bed, at my mercy. "Now, allow me to return the favour."

Her eyes widened at my low, sultry tone and I felt her heart flutter. She liked this side of me. Good. She was mine, to do with as I liked, and to worship for all time.

Kate wanted to say something, another witty comeback perhaps. She had quite a mouth on her, this one. But I kissed her before she could give the words voice. I kissed her hard and hungrily and our lips moved together in the way that would make her forget. It did the trick. No sooner did I claim her tongue than she melted beneath me and her eyes drifted closed. Kate was not the only one enjoying the embrace and I had to struggle to keep my attention fixed on the task of undoing her jeans, rather than lose myself in the sensation of her tongue on mine as she explored the lines of my fangs…

She gasped and tore her mouth away when my finger slid through her slick folds, hooking up to rub the place behind her already swollen clit. "Luci-oh!"

"Mmm Kate, you're already dripping." I purred as I raised myself up to look into her eyes.

I held the look as my finger delved deeper, my thumb rubbing slow circles around the tiny bundle of nerves, purposely denying any contact there. Kate arched, her hips circling, silently pleading for more while pushing her jeans down those long willowy legs. I continued to deny her any such contact.

"Lu-Lucian, please!" She gasped, thrashing her head in the mad desperation of a person purposely being denied that one thing their body craved. And so, I took pity on her and pushed a second digit into her warmth while I bore my thumb down on her clit.

The sudden contact had her bucking, writhing, and shattering around my fingers and I watched as, for the first time in her young life, she was undone by another person. It filled me with a sense of primitive pride. I'd done this to her. I'd taken this beautiful creature and, simply with a touch, had reduced her to a mumbling scattered pool of desire and sex.

I was sure I had never seen anything more beautiful in all of my undead life.

This lovely creature had the smell of a virgin. Usually, this would have deterred me. There was no sport in feeding on virgins. They didn't have the experience to play the game, too easy to overwhelm and bend to my will. And, for all the weight that was put upon virtue, innocence made the blood bland. Lust, debauchery, and all the other sins of the flesh gave flavour, and I liked my food well spiced, flavoursome and aged just right.

But something had risen inside me, something primal that demanded more, demanded I make her completely lose herself and surrender to me. Make her mine.

Slowly, easing my fingers from her as the waves of her release ebbed away, I divested her of her jeans and boots in a single move. Free of their confines, her legs opened for me as I settled myself at her entrance. She moaned as my renewed erection bumped her clit and she didn't protest as I pulled her top over her head, revealing her lush milky white breasts topped by stiff rosy peaks.

Settling over her, I took her lips again, only this time the kiss was much more tender as I pushed forward. In the wash of such an intense orgasm, I knew Kate would be ready and relaxed, and I was confident she would barely feel the sting of her lost virtue.

She stiffened at my entry, the feeling taking her by surprise, but then her body opened to me and I began to rock against her as I worked myself deeper. She was tight. Orgasm or no, she was a virgin and I knew that I needed to work her slowly or else risk hurting her in ways no woman should suffer. Yet the need to take her clawed at me and the delicious feeling of her plush inner walls wrapped around me drove me on.

"That's it, take me in." I moaned and tried to fend off the desire to cum right then and there as I withdrew almost completely. I held there with just my tip inside her, letting the feeling of emptiness consume her, then I plunged back in.

"Luci-oh, oh God! Yes!" she moaned, whimpering as my rough fingers rolled over her throbbing clit. "Please... don't... don't stop... " She leant up and laid hot open-mouthed kisses along my neck.

I groaned and ground into her. "Go on baby, ask me to fuck you...and I will." I murmured into her ear, rocking into her depths, then withdrew again. "Kate... God, you feel so good... yea, beg me to fuck you... "

"F-F-Fuck me," she whispered desperately, her blush deepening. The words didn't come easy to her, but she rolled her hips against mine, coaxing me on, as her nails scraped down my back. "Please...fuck me Lucian... I want it... I want-" She suddenly screamed out my name at the feeling of me going balls deep, filling her to the brim, and all conscious thought melted away into a white-hot sea of pleasure. "Oh my god... Lucian! Oh, it feels good...It feels so good!" She cried, kissing me again as I repeated the move again and again, each thrust sending waves of pleasure crashing over her.

I groaned at the sensations radiating through her tight confines, every sense overloading as her irresistible scent filled my head and made my mouth water. I had never held out this long before feeding and my thirst was growing by the second. I was starving, yet I fought my very nature, for this girl.

Kate pushed against me and rolled us over so that her body straddled mine. Placing her hands on my shoulders and planting her feet securely on the bed, she started to ride me, moving up and down my cock without a shred of modesty.

"Oh! Oh! Ohhh!" Kate moaned as she crashed down on my cock, causing me to penetrate deeper.

She was growing more comfortable on top, her strides quickly becoming longer and harder, an upwards glide, then a crashing down slam. "Uh-uh-uh-oh…Lucian! Oh, fuck!" She gasped, working her body along my length with increasing vigour as her hands slid up her body to fondle her breasts. The gentleness was gone and the sex-crazed beast inside the young woman had emerged.

I leant up and I moved my hands to her back and ran my fingers along her spine while kissing along her collarbone. I could smell fresh, young blood rushing through her veins and it only served to drive me on. "Faster," I ordered, and the command was met with Kate's body sliding at a rapid pace against my own. She let out long, loud moans every time I was fully encased inside her. I nibbled on her jawline, following its curve to the other side of her neck and suddenly, unable to help myself, I bit down, causing her to gasp.

"Yes-yes-yes-oh Lucian!!" Kate cried. "I'm gonna cum! Oh fuck, I'm gonna cum again!"

"No Kate! Not till I'm ready, we're going to cum together, my little rabbit!"

For Kate, that seemed to be the final straw. "Oh God, Lucian, bite me!"

It was as if time held its breath. "What?"

"Please…" Kate was shaking, her eyes pleading. "Turn me. I want… I want to be…"

"No." My voice was level and firm, brokering no argument. Then I softened, my fingers stroking her spine. "You're too young. You have no idea what you'd be giving up. I can't."

"I don't care! I want to give it all up. I want to forget, I can't take it anymore. I see their face's, Lucian. David and my parents. Will I see them in my dreams every night if you turn me? Will I hear them calling-"

"You'll never forget. They'll never leave you, they'll become an eternal part of you. You'll carry them with you, through the ages till the end of time." My next words were like stones in my heart. "But the pain will go."

She nodded. "Then do it. Take my pain away. Anything is better than this… I can't… I won't…Please!"

"You'll be my thrall." I declared. "My servant. Bound to my will and do my bidding till the end of days. Is this what you want?"

"Yes!" She panted, so hot, needy, and desperate, I almost gave in. "There's nothing left for me here. A vampire, your thrall... slave, I don't care. I can't go back. Take me any way you want. I'm yours!"

"There is no going back," I warned. This was her last chance to back out. Her final chance to come to her senses.

"I know."

"Good." I kissed her hard before crushing her to me and laying her down on the bed. My fangs plunged deep into her throat at the same time as I ground myself back into her depths. Orgasmic screams filled the room as I drank from Kate, savouring every drop of her sweet nectar as I drained her to the point where she had not a single drop of blood left within. Feeling her go limp in my arms, I felt a sudden stinging sensation stab at my throat as I cut my veins with a sharpened talon. I leant over and spilled my own blood into the woman's waiting mouth. "Everything I am is yours, and all you are is mine. Blood of my blood, flesh of my flesh. Together forever..."

I completed the bonding.

She died in my arms and was reborn, awakening to the world a fledgeling vampire, my thrall, my companion, and would grow to become the great love of my eternal life.

But that is a story for another time...

TEMPTATION JUST GOT EVEN SWEETER...
Sweet
Temptations:
THE BOSS'S DAUGHTER
THE LORD OF LUST
L.M. MOUNTFORD

He thought his temptations were over, but they were only just beginning...

Until last week, Richard Martin was just another middle-aged guy. Married to a wife he loved, father to a son he adored, stuck in a dead-end job, just counting the days go by...
Then everything changed.
He made a mistake.
Now to save his marriage, he's going to have to pay the price.
There's just one problem, Scarlet Holmes.
His Supervisor.
She loves to play games with her staff and now, seeming very aware of his little secret, she wants to play a game.
And she always gets what she wants.
Because she just so happens to be The Boss's Daughter.

FORBIDDEN
Desire
CONFESSIONS OF A TROPHY WIFE
BOOK 1
THE LORD OF LUST
L.M. MOUNTFORD

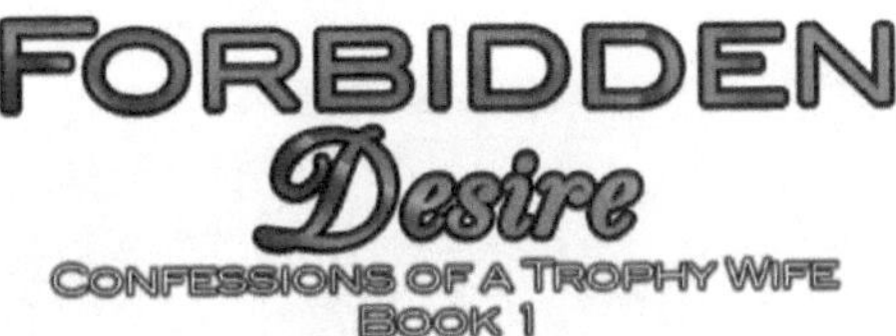

To all the rest of the world, Elizabeth Clarke has it all.
A successful husband. A beautiful home. And now a son off to
university. She is a perfect housewife with the perfect life.
It's a lie.
Her husband is a lying, drinking philanderer who hates her as much
as she loathes him. Her home is beautiful, but empty, nothing more
than a gilded cage to keep her trapped in a world she never wanted.
That is, until he came back into town.
Hugh Becket.
Her son's best friend. He's hot, young, and so forbidden.
Elizabeth knows she should stay away, but when the devil comes
knocking on her door in the middle of the night, what's a poor
neglected trophy wife to do?

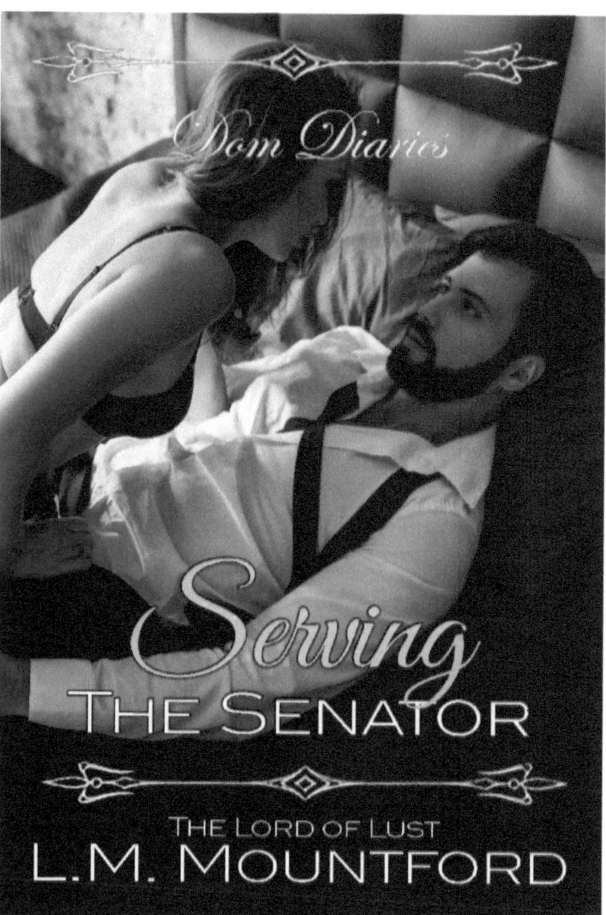

Dom Diaries
Serving
THE SENATOR
THE LORD OF LUST
L.M. MOUNTFORD

He is my Hades

I'd played the role of a goddess, bound and chained for the service of mortals.

He freed me.

He freed me, unchained me and taken me to his underworld, his dark realm where he'd brought out all my forbidden and secret desires.

And now I'm his.

His attendant. His servant…

Serving the Senator is a sizzling new release from the lord of Lust. Loaded with tension and sizzling chemistry, it is a modern reimagining of the ancient myth of Hades and Persephone. A stand-alone romance, it is loaded with scenes of an adult nature that feature BDSM, Dominance play, and so much heat, they may very well melt your e-reader…

DELICIOUSLY SINFUL
Liaisons

A COLLECTION OF HOT AND ORGASMIC STORIES
FROM THE LORD OF LUST

L.M. MOUNTFORD

DELICIOUSLY SINFUL LIAISONS

Deliciously Sinful Liaisons - A collection of hot and orgasmic stories by The Lord of Lust

-Broken
-Just Once
- Valentine Misadventures
-Together in Sydney
-Training Tracey
-Blood Lust
-Sweet Temptations

And for the first time ever, an extract from the lord's long-awaited and much-anticipated sequel to his debut - Sweet Temptations: The Boss's Daughter

Temptation And Seduction

L.M. MOUNTFORD

TEMPTATION & SEDUCTION

Five tales of Lust, desire & Temptation
L.M. Mountford, The Lord of Lust, brings you a collection of some of his hottest works. 5 of the sexiest stories ever released on Kindle & Ereader... Plus, for the first time ever, read an extract from the long-awaited sequel to his debut - Sweet Temptation: The Boss's Daughter

Just Once

Valentine Misadventures

Play Time: Extra Credit

Stepdaddy's Bad Girl

Sweet Temptations

REC
THEIR SILENCE COMES AT A PRICE...
UNCOVERED
THE LORD OF LUST
L.M. MOUNTFORD

UNCOVERED
L. M. MOUNTFORD

When Mina returns for her stepbrother's 21st birthday, she thinks her days of lusting after him are over. Caught up in the heat and passion of the moment, she is stunned to find them back in bed together; their feelings clearly far from resolved. Haunted by her desire, and her growing appetite for , Mina now has another problem… she must head down a path of lust and desire; torn between the dark delights of the handsome bad boy down the street and her adorable stepbrother who has always been there for her. Can she confront the truth she has long tried to bury? How far will she go to save the one she wants but knows she can never truly have?

Together In
SYDNEY
LM Mountford

They were the best of friends. Then they shared a night of passion and in the morning she was gone.

Alex has spent years trying to forget his first love. But then an email arrives out of the blue and suddenly he finds himself boarding the first plane bound for Australia with nothing but his passport and an overnight bag. He's no idea what he'll do, or he's going to say, but one thing's for sure. He's not going home without her.

Time may heal all wounds. But the heart never mends easy.

Childhood lovers reunite on the sun-kissed beaches of Sydney Australia, yet will their reunion spark a holiday fling or summer storm?

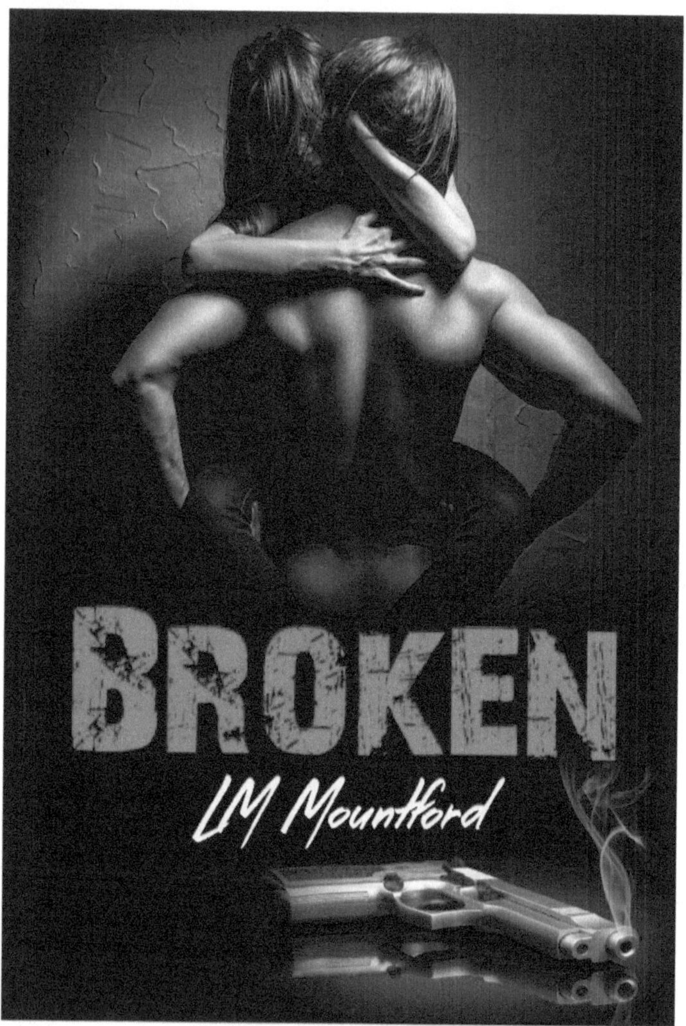
BROKEN
LM Mountford

BROKEN

Vickey Romano is the girl with a secret you don't want to bring home to mum.
Beautiful, haunted, and on the run, she works a string of temp jobs and never lets anyone get too close. Until that is, she meets Jake. The living definition of dark and dangerous, he tells her nothing about himself, keeps a SIG P226 in his bedside table and can make her go weak-kneed with just a word.
She knows she should stay away, he has her caught in his web and she's helpless to resist.
All she can do is hope her past doesn't kill him in the process...

Play Time
Books 1&2
DARK INFERNO

Play Time
Books 1 & 2

Play Time: Double Period combines Naughty Students, Magic Girls &
Demonic Succubus Teachers that will suck you dry and leave you begging
for another round.

Here both the titillating Paranormal Erotica Hit and it's sequel, Extra Credit
are available like never before in a 30,000+ word lesson in submission,
BDSM and Fem Domination that will have you hooked page after page.

THEY'LL TEACH
THEIR DAUGHTER'S
BEST FRIEND A
LESSON SHE WILL
NEVER FORGET...

TRAINING
Tracey

TRAINING TRACEY

Tracey has known the Burtons practically all her life. They're her best friend's parents. When she was a little girl they took her on days out to the beach. But she's a woman now, and they have some very important lessons to teach her...

** Training Tracey is A wicked and uber-hot coming-of-age ménage, filled with MF, FF & MFF scenes from the Lord of Lust's Dark and Dirty alter ego. There is NO cheating, NO cliff-hanger and a guaranteed HEA with plenty of steam.**

WARNING 18+: This book is erotic and contains material that may be considered offensive to some readers, which includes graphic language, explicit sex, and adult situations.

Just Once
A FRIENDS TO LOVERS ROMANCE
L.M. MOUNTFORD

JUST ONCE

They were the very poster children for the boy and girl next door, if a couple of streets apart.

Friends for longer than forever. They'd walked to school together. He'd protected her from the bullies when they teased her about her glasses. She'd tended to his cuts and bruises when he fell. He pushed her to try new things. She snuck looks at him when he wasn't looking.

All her life, Faye had loved Terry, but he was oblivious. He's her best friend, her closest friend, but he's oblivious and now he has a Girlfriend. All day long, she has to watch them together and it's killing her. She wants him, all of him, but he's taken. So, instead, she wants one night. Just once, one night, between friends.

One night, just once...